MARC
MAJEWSKI

DOES
EARTH
FEEL?

KATHERINE TEGEN BOOKS
An Imprint of HarperCollinsPublishers

Does Earth feel alive?

Does Earth feel calm?

Does Earth feel content?

Does Earth feel rested?

Does Earth feel curious?

Does Earth feel friendly?

Does Earth feel lonely?

Does Earth feel hurt?

Does Earth feel tired?

Does Earth feel sick?

Does Earth feel heard?

Does Earth feel protected?

Does Earth feel loved?

And you, what do you want Earth to feel?

Author's Note

How do we know Earth feels?

One of our greatest strengths as humans is our capacity to empathize with one another. That means we can feel what the other feels.

When I see a forest going up in smoke, I feel the flames myself. When I gaze upon the moon's reflection on a lake, I feel as calm as the still waters. It is empathy that connects us and allows for compassion and love. We cannot fully understand what we do not feel.

We often practice empathy for other humans, but we forget that we are also part of a larger family. From delicate spiders to big elephants, and within lush jungles and the deepest seas, we are all Earth—dependent on one another for survival. This fragile balance has been endangered by our lack of love and knowledge.

This is our only home. The time is now to honor Earth's natural past, open our eyes to the present, and protect the future for those still to come.

Will you join me?

To my family—M.M.

ISBN 978-0-06-302153-2

The artist used Acrylic paints on canvas to create
the illustrations for this book.
Typography by Chelsea C. Donaldson
20 21 22 23 24 SCP 10 9 8 7 6 5 4 3 2 1
❖
First Edition

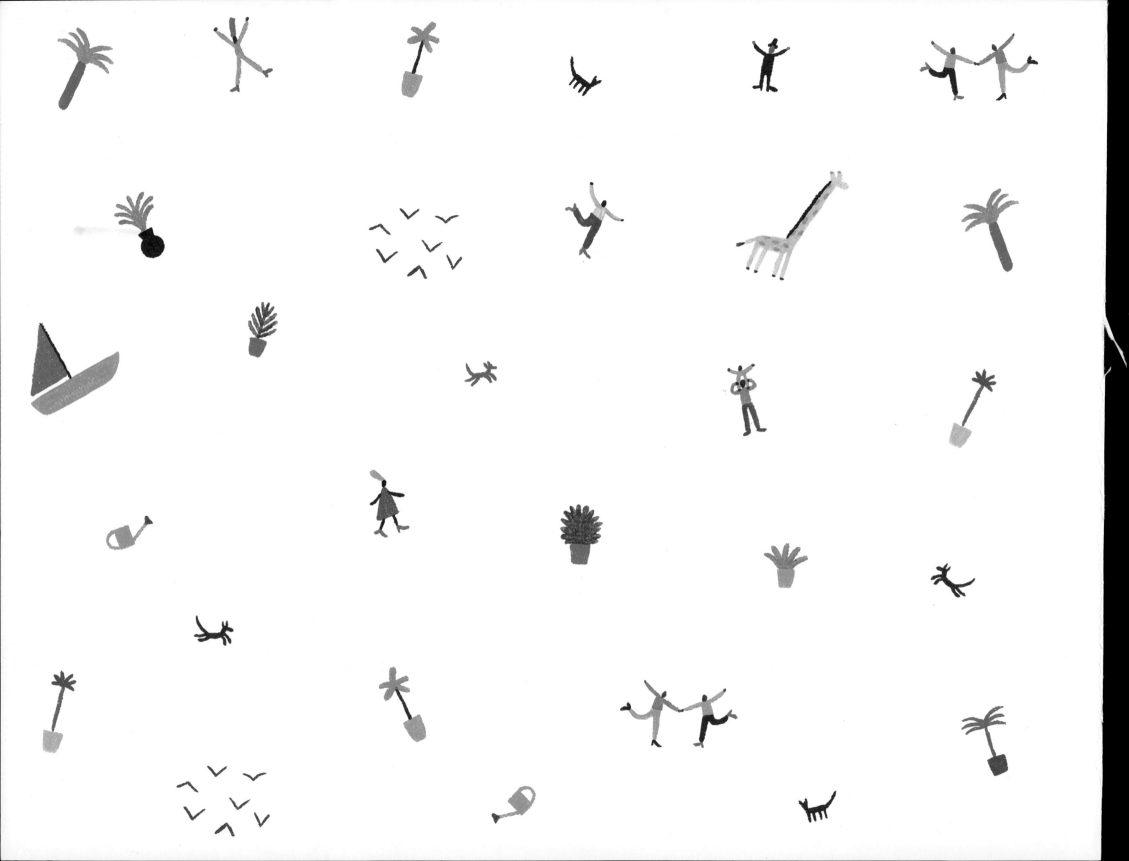